Contents

Chapter 1 All boys can help 7

BONUS Scrap metal 20

Chapter 2 The kings 23

BONUS At the pictures 36

Chapter 3 Changing fortunes 39

BONUS Food rationing 54

Chapter 4 Arch-enemy 57

BONUS Gas masks 70

Chapter 5 Off the rails 73

BONUS A map of Tedbury 86

Chapter 6 A will of iron 89

BONUS Wartime women 104

About the author 106

About the illustrator 108

Book chat 110

Chapter 1

All boys can help

"Give me that!"

Peggy jumped as Arthur snatched the poster away from her. She had been absorbed in looking at the pictures of a warship, tanks and massive guns on wheels. In big red capital letters at the top of the poster were the words **WEAPONS FROM SCRAP METAL**.

"Can't you *read?*" asked Arthur, jabbing his finger at the bottom of the poster and curling his lip. "What does it say?"

"Weapons ... from ... scrap ... metal," Peggy read.

"Not that bit, you clot!" said Bill, her elder brother. "The bit at the bottom."

"It saaaays," Arthur went on, slowly, like she was a baby, "All boys can help. All *boys* can help. Not girls. Me and Bill, we're going to get enough metal to build a whole tank."

"Why can't girls help?" asked Peggy.

"Because you couldn't pick up three teaspoons with your twiggy arms," said Bill.

Peggy chewed on one of her plaits and stared down at her arms. They were a bit skinny, maybe, but she could pick up a whole basket of wet laundry on her own. That was pretty heavy.

"Girls should be able to help, too!" Peggy said.

"You can help," said Mother, "by peeling some potatoes. Your brothers are going out to support the war effort. They need a good meal inside them."

Peggy sighed. She got peeling, putting each skinned potato into a saucepan of water while Mother put two lumps of something pink and shiny into an oven tray. Peggy shuddered. Not sheep's hearts *again*. She hated sheep's hearts.

"You can wipe that look off your face," said Mother. "If you're too dainty for sheep's heart, you can give your share to your brothers. It's good food for growing lads, that is."

"Can me and Jed go out and look for metal, too?" asked Peggy. She put down her potato peeler and set the pan on the stove. "We want to win the prize."

Mother laughed. "You and Jed?"

The competition had got everyone excited. Whoever brought the most metal to the steps of Tedbury Parish Hall on Saturday would win a medal and a ten-shilling note, presented by Lady Farrington. They would also get a ride in a tank. An *actual* tank called *Matilda II*. Arthur and Bill had been talking about it all week.

Peggy thought calling a tank *Matilda* was peculiar. Even odder was another tank called *Valentine*.

Matilda and Valentine sounded like they should be waltzing around the dance floor instead of firing at enemy soldiers.

"We might not win," Peggy admitted. She wasn't a *total* clot. She knew her big, strong brothers would go marching around the streets in their Scout uniforms and charm every spare bit of metal from everyone who opened their door.

"We just want to help," she said.

Mother snorted. "You've enough helping to do at home, young lady."

Peggy *did* give her sheep's heart to her brothers. She knew it was good food, but she just hated the way it felt between her teeth – like biting into an old rubber ball. She ate her carrots, potatoes and mashed turnip with Mother's thin gravy.

Her brothers bolted their food down at high speed. They tore out into the afternoon on their mission to gather a mountain of scrap iron, copper, aluminium and lead.

After she'd washed and dried all the pots and dishes, Peggy slipped out, too. Mother was in the back yard, pushing wet clothes through the mangle, and didn't notice.

Peggy ran towards the woods, crossing the humpbacked bridge that spanned the railway and slip-sliding down the steep bank to the wire fence that ran beside the tracks. She found Jed there, in his usual scruffy jumper and baggy shorts. He was peering intently through the chain-link.

"You look like you're at the pictures, watching Flash Gordon!" she laughed.

"Think how many tanks you could make with those railway tracks," said Jed.

"But then we couldn't go anywhere on the train," Peggy pointed out.

"True," said Jed, rubbing a hand through his tufty brown hair. "But I reckon we might find some old metal along the fence."

"Good idea," said Peggy. "Let's look."

They searched beside the fence, kicking through weeds and gravel. Within a few minutes they'd found some old shelf brackets, lots of bottle-tops and a bent, rusty bike wheel.

They put these in an old sack Jed had brought. Looking at the bottle-tops made Peggy feel thirsty.

"I wish we had some lemonade," she sighed. It was a warm day. She took her cardigan off and tied the arms around her waist.

"I can't remember when I last drank lemonade," said Jed, and she felt bad. Jed lived in a tiny house near the woods. His mum was dead and his dad had been injured by a bomb and now he couldn't work. Jed didn't get much to eat. He certainly got no lemonade. He was even skinnier than she was.

Beyond the fence, the tracks began to vibrate. All at once, a locomotive went thundering past, with a long cloud of sooty smoke billowing in its wake.

"Look!" Jed pointed up the bank. The brambles were getting flattened by the gust from the train, revealing a pale blue curve and a tangle of spokes. They scrambled closer and both hooted with delight when they spotted the words 'Silver Cross'.

"A pram! A whole pram!" cried Peggy. "That's heaps of metal!"

But just as she reached out to grab it, there was a sharp thud on her shoulder. She gave a little shriek as a small lump of red brick dropped into the leaves.

"Ow!" Jed was rubbing his elbow and spinning around to stare angrily along the bank beside the railway line.

A small knot of figures stood at the bend. "Oi!" one of them shouted. "That's our pram, that is! We found it first!"

"It's NOT yours!" yelled Peggy. "*We* just found it!" She recognised Gary Smedley and Richie Carter, older boys from school, with two other boys she didn't know.

"We found it yesterday and we're coming back for it," said Gary. "So you two can clear off, or else." He raised his hand and threw a lump of wood towards them. It smashed into the pram and rebounded into the weeds. A cloud of thistledown rose up in protest.

"Leave us alone!" Peggy yelled, tugging angrily at the pram and ripping it through the brambles with snaps and cracks.

Jed picked up the bit of wood, getting ready to throw it back, but Peggy could see it was hopeless. They were outnumbered.

BONUS
Scrap metal

Recycling is not a new thing. Back in the 1940s, during the Second World War, Britain desperately needed metal to help build new tanks, warships and guns.

Posters went up to encourage people to help the war effort by collecting as much metal as possible. Boy Scouts, in particular, were urged to get out and gather all they could.

People also collected paper, cloth, rubber – and even animal bones left over from cooking, for making glue and explosives.

The poster Peggy saw is based on a real poster from that time. It did say 'ALL BOYS CAN HELP'.

Why do you think girls weren't included?

Chapter 2

The kings

There was a shout and two tall figures came down the bank. "Wanna pick on someone your own size?" yelled a familiar voice.

Bill and Arthur hurtled towards Gary's gang who immediately turned and fled.

Peggy felt mixed up. On the one hand, it was nice to have her big brothers come to her rescue. On the other hand, now they would tease her even more about being little and weak.

"What are you doing here?" demanded Arthur, as they walked back.

"Getting metal!" said Peggy. "We found this!"

Bill's eyebrows went up. He took hold of the pram and wrenched it out of the brambles with one strong tug. "Good find," he said, nodding towards Jed. "That'll help."

Then he and Arthur climbed back up the bank, carrying the pram between them.

"Wait!" Jed shouted after them. "*We* found that!"

"Well done," called back Arthur, laughing. "We'll put a label on it to say it was you."

And all Peggy could do was stand there, speechless, as her brothers marched off back to the road with *their* find.

"They weren't rescuing us," she said. "They were just rescuing the metal." She felt a heavy, cold lump settle inside her at the unfairness of it all.

Jed said nothing for a few moments. Then he picked up their sack of the brackets, the wheel and the beer bottle-tops. "We've still got these," he said.

Peggy stamped furiously up the steep bank, grabbing hold of roots and branches to haul herself up. She wanted to start looking somewhere fresh. Jed climbed after her, puffing, with the sack over his shoulder.

At the top was an area of straggly trees, and beyond these was a neglected patch of land beneath the high brick wall surrounding the Farrington Estate. Beyond the walls were the lawns, ponds and flower beds of the grand old house owned by Lord and Lady Farrington.

The people of Tedbury got to see inside the grounds every May when the Farrington family opened their high wrought-iron gates and put on a summer fete for the village.

Today, though, Peggy and Jed were very much on the outside as they trudged through knee-high clumps of ragwort and thistle, scanning the ground for anything that glinted or gleamed.

Jed suddenly gave a shout. "Look!" He pointed to a wobbly panel of corrugated iron which lay across a boggy area next to some gorse hedges.

It was as big as a garden gate. Peggy ran over to Jed, feeling her boots slide as she hauled up her end of it.

The iron made squelching sounds as it emerged from the mud. It was much heavier than it looked.

"Careful!" yelled Jed. "Be careful, Peg!" Because the tilted metal was buckling and he was losing his grip.

Abruptly, it slipped from Jed's grasp and swung over, toppling Peggy with a wallop and a dull ringing sound. She found herself face down in a soup of earth, rust and weeds, pinned flat by iron.

"Peggy!" yelled Jed, his voice sounding fearful.

"It's all right," she called back. "I'm fine. Just – " She had been about to say 'get it off me' but the words suddenly deserted her, as she stared into the soggy earth beneath her chin.

She could see a man's ear.

She put out a finger and scraped some soil off the ear, revealing a jaw and the side of a nose.

"Jed – " she murmured, as her friend lugged the iron panel off her backside. "I've just found the king."

"You, what?" said Jed.

"King George!" Peggy sat up, heedless of the mud now seeping into her dress. She stared at the gleaming silver coin in her left hand. The image of King George the Sixth gazed serenely towards her thumb.

"A half-crown," marvelled Jed, crouching down beside her. "I wasn't expecting that kind of metal!"

"There's another!" Peggy leaned forward and dug out a second muddy coin.

"There could be more," breathed Jed, excitedly scanning the ground. He pulled one of the shelf brackets out of his sack and used it to dig into the soil. Excited, Peggy took out the other one and did the same. They scored deep grooves through the mud and, over the next ten minutes, turned up another three half-crowns.

"Four half-crowns! That's ten shillings!" marvelled Peggy. "Imagine what we could buy with ten shillings!" She suddenly stopped, remembering the empty larder she'd noticed last time she'd been in Jed's house.

Her eyes swept across his feet, at the boots which had a hole cut across the toes because his feet had outgrown them. She glanced at the two coins in her hands and then passed them to her friend.

"Get some boots. And some food," she said.

Jed stared at her, going pink across his freckled cheeks. "I'm not taking it all! We'll take half each," he said.

"But you need boots. And food," said Peggy. "More than me."

"Half each," repeated Jed, staring at her with a steely expression.

"Fine. Half each," she sighed, taking the coins back. She wondered if Mother might spend some of it on a whole chicken instead of sheep's hearts.

"I reckon that's all of it," said Jed. "Someone dropped their wages, I reckon. But we'll never know who, so it's not as if we can give it back."

"We should get the iron," said Peggy. "If we can carry it." She leaned on one end of her shelf bracket as she got up. And then she felt, rather than heard, a kind of grating deep in the dug-out soil beneath it. "Wait," she said. "I think there might be one more half-crown!"

They both leaned into the hole they had made and saw not a round coin shape but a metal corner.

"What's that?" murmured Jed, using his bracket again to scrape the heavy, dark soil away.

"It's a box," said Peggy, feeling excitement stirring once more.

She was right. Digging together, they gradually unearthed a small chest, made of wood but with metal corners. It was about the size of a shoebox and had a curved lid. The lock on its front knocked off easily with one strike of Jed's bracket.

Inside, they found scrunched up newspaper. Beneath the newspaper was a gleaming puddle of half-crowns – and beneath the coins, a layer of one-pound notes.

Jed stared at Peggy and Peggy stared at Jed. They were speechless, but not just because of this incredible amount of money.

Set into the inner curve of the lid was a piece of paper, sealed against the old wood with red wax. On it were the words:

TAKE THIS AND I WILL COME FOR YOU.

BONUS
At the pictures

What's half a crown worth?

In 1942 half a crown would buy 200 grams of butter, 300 grams of sugar, or 100 grams of cheese. These foods were quite expensive during the war, though, and you could only have small amounts, using a ration book to make sure you didn't get more than your fair share.

Half a crown today would be worth about £5. So half a crown would buy you a meal deal in a supermarket today.

Or you could maybe go to a special Saturday morning club at the cinema. During the war the cinema (or 'the pictures' as many people called cinemas) meant a lot to people. Nobody had a television or any kind of screen time at home.

Popular short films for children at the Saturday morning cinema clubs included exciting series like *Flash Gordon* or *The Lone Ranger*. There would be cartoons, too, and weekly shows about cowboys and detectives.

You could stay and watch all morning for just sixpence. Half a crown would buy a ticket for you and four friends.

Chapter 3

Changing fortunes

They could have reburied the box.

The warning was clear. ***Take this and I will come for you.***

"But how would anyone *know* who's taken it?" asked Peggy, twirling one plait around her muddy fingers.

"This one's dated 1942," said Jed, taking a coin. "So this box hasn't been here long."

"Let's go somewhere and count it," said Peggy. "Then we can decide what to do."

They put the box into the sack. It weighed a lot now, so they carried it between them.

"If anyone asks, it's just lots of old tins and bottle-tops," said Peggy.

But the only interruption to their journey was a red motorcar that drove over the railway bridge so fast it had to skid to a halt to avoid hitting them.

"A Triumph Roadster!" squawked Jed, as he cannoned into the bridge wall.

"Look out, you idiots!" shouted the driver who wore a silk scarf and a boater hat. "What on earth are you doing?!"

In the back seat, a brown-haired boy around Bill's age stared at them with a smirk.

"We're getting metal for the war effort," Peggy called back, indignantly. "And you might say sorry!"

"Does it really go at 80 miles an hour?" asked Jed, too fascinated by the motorcar to be annoyed.

The man barked a laugh and turned to look at his son. "Does it, Edmund?"

"You bet it does," said the boy.

Then the car took off again, roaring up the hill and turning sharply in between the high open gates of the big house.

Jed stared, awestruck. "Maybe we've got enough to buy one," he murmured.

"But neither of us can drive," Peggy pointed out.

They cut across the woods to get back to Jed's house.

"Dad's helping at the farm," said Jed, leading Peggy through the overgrown back garden. "As much as he can, with his bad leg."

After getting injured, Jed's dad had lost his job as a dairy deliveryman. He took what work he could get. His son's thin face and worn clothes were evidence there wasn't enough money coming in.

Even Peggy's mother, always grumbling about having to stretch Father's Army wage, sometimes gave Jed some bread and dripping. She said he looked like a scarecrow.

Jed waded through weeds towards the Anderson air raid shelter where he and his father hid whenever the bombers flew over. Inside, it was dark and damp, with just a Tilley lamp for light. *Air raids couldn't be much fun in there*, thought Peggy.

Inside the hut, it was too gloomy to see properly. Jed found a box of matches on a low shelf and lit the lamp, filling the shelter with a hissing golden light.

They emptied the box and began to count. There were 72 half-crowns, which they stacked up in fives. Next came the notes. Peggy stared in wonder at a flimsy rectangle of blue and pink paper with the words *Bank of England: I promise to pay the bearer on demand the sum of one pound.*

There were 22 one-pound notes.

"Including the half-crowns, that's … 32 pounds!" breathed Peggy.

Jed stared at the pile of money as if he expected it to suddenly burst into flames. Peggy understood why. How could this possibly be *real*? Mother had once told her Father's wages were five pounds a week. So … this was over *six weeks' wages*.

"So … 16 pounds each," said Jed.

They sat in awed silence.

Eventually, Peggy said: "Are we allowed?"

Jed said: "Finders, keepers … losers, weepers."

Peggy pointed to the words inside the box lid. "That doesn't sound like someone who's just going to weep."

Jed shrugged. "If they wanted to keep it safe, they shouldn't have buried it in a bog."

"But should we take it to the police?" asked Peggy.

"Let's sleep on it," Jed suggested. "Hide it for now and decide what to do tomorrow."

With the box pushed under the shelf, deep in the shadows, they walked back out to the street, trying to be normal.

"We should go back. Get that corrugated iron," said Peggy. "We have to try and beat Arthur and Bill."

"I'm famished, though," said Jed. Then, winking, he pulled a single half-crown from his pocket. "Let's go to the cake shop."

Minutes later, they were eating huge slabs of spicy bread pudding as they walked. "Mrs Bassett thought I'd got the half-crown for my birthday," said Jed.

In the woods, he sorted out the shillings and pennies he'd got in change, and gave half to Peggy. The coins chinked quietly in her cardigan pocket.

"Wooooo-hoooo!" Jed suddenly started running and jumping and thwacking at low twigs. Peggy joined in, whooping and bounding all the way to the stream. She skipped lightly across the old plank bridge. Jed, though, had forgotten that if you trod too heavily in the wrong place the whole thing tipped. He got tipped just before he reached the bank and dropped, with a splosh, into the stream.

"We need to put some old bricks under that or something," he puffed as they walked on. Peggy could hear his socks squelching. Jed was still grinning, though.

But back beneath the Farrington Estate wall, a shock awaited them. An hour ago, they had carefully filled in the hole and dropped the iron panel back over it. Now the panel was flung away and the hole was back. Deeper and wider than before, as if it had been properly excavated with a spade. Peggy suddenly felt cold inside.

"They came back," she whispered. "They came back for the treasure and found it gone."

Jed stared around, gnawing his lower lip. "Come on," he said. "Let's just get our iron and go."

In silence, they picked up the panel and walked away, carrying it flat between them. They had agreed to take it to Jed's house to avoid Arthur or Bill stealing it. It was awkward and heavy. They kept needing to rest.

As they reached the humpbacked bridge, the metal was digging hard into Peggy's palms and leaving rusty stains on her dress, to go with all the mud. Mother would be furious. Maybe she would be less furious if Peggy presented her with 16 pounds. Or maybe she would be *more* furious. It was hard to guess.

She somehow doubted that Arthur or Bill would have such worries if *they* ever found 16 pounds. Finding treasure was exactly what Boy Scouts were supposed to do. Keeping the house clean and the potatoes peeled was exactly what their sisters were supposed to do.

This was what she was thinking, when there was a tremendous crash and she found herself flipping like an acrobat through the air.

BONUS
Food rationing

During the Second World War, some foods were hard to get. Flour, eggs and sugar had to be rationed so there was enough to go round everyone.

People found clever ways to make cakes with what they had. Bread pudding was made with leftover bread (sometimes a bit stale), currants or raisins, sweet spices, butter, margarine or lard, powdered egg (if you couldn't get a real one) and just a little sugar (if you could get some).

Bread and dripping was another snack. It was the fat left in a pan after some meat had been cooked, spread onto bread.

Ration books were given to every household and were stamped in shops each time rationed food was bought. You had to show your ration book to prove you hadn't already had your allowance for that week. It was a way to share things out fairly.

What food would you miss if there was rationing?

Chapter 4

Arch-enemy

"Where is it?" hissed a voice.

Peggy was dazed. There was a damp, earthy smell and a heavy weight on her knees.

"Wake up!" The voice sounded muffled and odd. "Tell me where you hid it!"

Peggy blinked and saw staring, glassy eyes and a long black snout, punctured with several nostrils. She shrieked.

"Be quiet, kid!" The snout shook. "Or you'll be in a lot of trouble."

He had an American accent – like Flash Gordon, the hero of the short films at Saturday Morning Cinema Club.

This was no hero, though, and no alien from Planet Mongo. It was someone wearing a gas mask. Peggy thought he looked like an older boy, not a man.

"Don't scream!" he hissed, blue eyes blinking behind round discs of glass set into rubber. "Just tell me where you put that box."

Overhead was a sooty brick arch. Peggy lay on the bank above the tracks, beneath the road bridge. She vaguely remembered the metal panel jerking, tipping her over. She must have tumbled right down the grassy slope. The panel lay across her legs.

"Where's Jed?" she croaked.

"Over there," said Gas Mask Boy. "He won't tell me where my money is."

Jed was slumped against the brick arch, one foot out in front of him. He looked grey.

"What have you done to him?!" gasped Peggy.

"Nothing!" snapped Gas Mask Boy. "I don't hurt little kids. You both fell down the bank and he's busted his ankle. *I* didn't do anything."

"But you're not here to help us," she said.

"Look, kid," he grunted. "I know you dug up my money. Didn't you read the warning in the box? I come after thieves."

"We're not thieves," argued Peggy. "We found it. We're going to take it to the police," she added, stoutly. And not quite truthfully.

"Oh no, you're not." He flipped the iron panel off her legs and hauled her to her feet. "You're gonna show me exactly where you hid it."

"Get *off*!" Peggy shook free and ran across to Jed.

"Sorry," Jed said, in a thin voice. "The car came over the bridge really fast and I jumped and the panel twisted … then we both went over and down the bank. Then this joker came running down in his flamin' gas mask, shouting about the money."

Peggy glared at Gas Mask Boy. "He needs help."

"Sure, he does," said Gas Mask Boy. "But not until you show me where you hid my money."

Peggy stared at him. "Why are you wearing that stupid mask? Are you trying to be scary?"

Gas Mask Boy sighed and the glass eyeholes briefly steamed up. "It's better for you if you don't know who I am," he said, in a low, dramatic voice. "Just give me the money and then you can come back and look after your friend."

"Don't go anywhere with him," grunted Jed, trying to move his swollen ankle to a more comfortable position.

"Just leave us alone," said Peggy.

"Nope. Not until I get my money back," said Gas Mask Boy. "It's lucky for you I don't go round hurting little kids. But that doesn't mean you're getting away with it. Take me to my money now … or I'll find out where you live. And I'll send someone round to collect what's owed to me … a bad guy who won't care if you're a kid."

Jed groaned. "I think my ankle's broken," he said.

Peggy glanced around, hoping someone might come and help, but there was nobody about.

That cold sinking feeling was back again.

Of *course* they couldn't keep the money. Why on earth had she ever thought they could? Poor, unimportant children never got money. Like the pram, it was just going to be taken off them by somebody bigger and more powerful.

She got up and followed Gas Mask Boy out of the shadow of the railway bridge.

"Right. How far is it?" he asked.

"It's a short walk," she muttered. "Along the road and – "

"We're not going on the road. That's gonna look suspicious. You'd better know a way through the woods and fields."

"It's through there," said Peggy, pointing to the woods on the far side of the tracks. She did not want to walk anywhere with this boy; she needed to get this job done, hand back the money and get Jed to a doctor.

"Right ... so, we'll cross the bridge and go that way, through the trees," Gas Mask Boy said.

He climbed back up the grassy bank, checking there was nobody about on the road. A black Austin Ten motorcar was badly parked just before the bridge.

"Did you drive here in that?" she asked.

"You bet," said Gas Mask Boy.

"But you're not old enough!"

"Says who?" said Gas Mask Boy.

Grabbing her wrist, he led her back down the bank on the far side of the bridge. "Don't try anything stupid," he said. "If you run away, you'll be sorry. I'll find out where you live and that bad guy ... he'll come knocking."

"I'm not the one being stupid," muttered Peggy.

"Watch your mouth, kid," snapped Gas Mask Boy.

But remembering that earlier journey gave Peggy an idea. The idea sent prickles up her spine ... and a sudden surge of determination. She'd had *enough* of being shoved around. Maybe, just *maybe*, she could do a little shoving of her own ...

This journey through the woods was very different to the last. Excitement and whooping had turned to dread and muttering.

Gas Mask Boy clearly didn't know these woods. He would have no clue where she was taking him.

So she led him on a wide, circular route, until they reached the plank bridge over the stream.

"You'll have to let me go," she said. "I need both arms to balance!"

"All right – but don't you run," he warned, releasing her. "Or you and your friend will be sorry."

Peggy rubbed her wrist, glaring up at him. Then she turned and skipped lightly across the plank, landing her feet in exactly the right places.

Gas Mask Boy followed without a thought. His shiny shoes hit the plank at exactly the place Peggy had hoped for. The plank tipped sideways, and he waved his arms wildly in the air as he pitched over. He might still have made it across, but Peggy gave her end of the plank a quick hard kick and it dropped into the water, taking the flailing boy with it.

The stream was no more than knee-deep but he fell right under. A loud splash was followed by angry, spluttering curses.

Peggy didn't wait to see or hear any more. She ran.

BONUS
Gas masks

Every child in the country had to have a gas mask with them at certain times during the Second World War. Schools all over the country ran lessons on how to quickly put them on in case of gas attack. They would be put on quickly if enemy planes dropped poisonous gas bombs.

Happily, there was never a gas attack in Britain.

But the masks would be a good disguise, because it was hard to see anyone's face once they had put one on. Still, it wouldn't be fun for very long, because gas masks were hot and smelly and uncomfortable.

Chapter 5

Off the rails

If there was one thing Peggy *was* good at it was running. Her brothers were bigger and stronger, but she was faster. She and Jed spent a lot of time chasing around the fields and woods of Tedbury, and even though Jed, too, was pretty fast, Peggy always won the races.

She might be small, but her limbs were wiry and quick. Also, she knew these fields and woods very well. Before Gas Mask Boy had even staggered, dripping, to his feet, she was out of sight. Soon she was well away from the stream, glancing fleetingly at him from behind a tree. She heard him bellow with rage as she turned and ran on, her feet light and almost noiseless in the soft summer leaf litter. His own angry crashing through the trees would mask any sound she might make.

He called out a few times, yelling: "Kid! Hey, kid! You'd better come back!" He must have taken off the gas mask so he could be heard. Strangely, he sounded different ... not so ... American.

But soon she was too far away to hear him. Minutes later, she was hurtling back down towards the bank of the railway, so fast that she whacked against the chain-link fence. Beyond it, on the far side of the tracks, she could see Jed still sitting by the railway bridge, his eyes squeezed shut with pain.

She could see a gap in the fence that some of the stupider children sometimes squeezed through. She knew never to go onto the tracks. But if, just this *once*, she went through and ran across, she would have more time to get Jed away before Gas Mask Boy caught up with them.

Even as she thought this, there was a terrific SCREEEEEEEAM and a massive punch of air. A locomotive suddenly shot through the archway beneath the bridge, steam belching out of its engine, roaring like a rampaging metal beast.

She found herself thrown backwards onto the rough ground by the blast wave. She lay there, gasping and shaking, as carriage after carriage thundered past. As soon as the last carriage was gone, she leaped to her feet, her legs shaking violently, and staggered up the bank to the bridge, steam rising around her.

Up on the road, she could see the black Austin car was still at the verge on the far side of the bridge, where she and Jed had tumbled over. She ran past it, too scared to look back, because she could hear Gas Mask Boy shouting again. She hoped the drifting cloud of sooty steam would hide her from his sight.

"What's happening? Where is he?" squawked Jed, as Peggy climbed down the bank and ran to him.

"Quick!" she said. "We haven't got much time. I dunked him in the stream and got away, but he won't be far behind."

She helped Jed up and he winced with pain.

"You'll have to hop," she said. "Lean on me. We'll get back up onto the road and then go to Farrington House," she said. "There will be people there."

"Well, we'd better go soon," said Jed. "Listen."

Through the trees beyond the tracks came a not so distant yell: "KID! Hey, KID! Where are you? I'm warning you ... you'd better come back!"

Like partners in a three-legged race, they ran and hopped to the far underside of the bridge, to get out of sight as quickly as possible. Just as they scrambled up past the corner of the brick arch, Peggy caught a glimpse of the boy emerging through the trees, putting his gas mask back on.

They clambered onto the road, past the Austin, and began to run and hop along as fast as possible.

"I think he was driving that car," puffed Peggy. "Although he *can't* be old enough!" Poor Jed was puffing and sweating, trying hard not to whimper. Peggy put her arm under his shoulder and propelled him. The road was uphill and soon Gas Mask Boy would crest the bank onto the bridge and be able to see them clearly in the distance. Well ... they would just have to outrun and out-hop him!

The high brick pillars and tall black wrought-iron gates of Farrington House were about 30 seconds away from them.

"Don't stop! We're nearly there!" Peggy gasped, dizzy from the effort of keeping herself and Jed moving so fast while her heart felt like it was doing cartwheels of panic.

Glancing back, she saw a familiar figure on the road. "Nearly there!" she gasped, as they reached the imposing entrance to the grounds of Farrington House.

Except they *weren't* nearly there – because the driveway went on and on. It would take them three or four minutes to reach the house, passing through its rolling, perfectly maintained green lawns and gardens. And now a fearful noise rose above their huffing and puffing – the sound of an engine, getting closer and closer.

As they passed the gates, they could hear the motorcar gaining speed behind them. Would the driver dare to come right into the grounds? Could they run and hide in the shrubs and bushes?

That wasn't so easy, because on either side of the long gravel driveway were metres and metres of decorative wrought-iron railings, with many curls and twists and little black metal roses. These railings ran all the way to the front of the house. Peggy thought maybe *she* could leap over and run but she knew Jed couldn't …

She heard the Austin getting closer as she dragged Jed along with her, yelling: "Hurry! Hurry!"

She realised it had been one long day of dangerous metal. First the pram, causing the missile-hurling before her brothers stepped in, then the iron panel falling on her, then the coins which had brought so much mayhem, then the railway tracks and her close brush with a huge iron locomotive … and finally, this car, bearing down on them.

"STOP!"

A tall woman suddenly stepped out across the driveway, holding up a gloved hand and glaring … but not at Peggy and Jed. Her gaze was directed over their heads, at the motorcar which was now squealing to a halt.

Peggy and Jed fell to their knees, panting. Towering over them was the elegant figure of Lady Farrington, a basket of cut roses over her arm and a small pair of garden shears in one hand. The other hand was still raised firmly at the driver, as she stared at him in fury.

"Edmund!" she shouted. "Stop the engine and get out of that car. And take that ridiculous mask off. RIGHT NOW."

Chapter 6

A will of iron

"Do have some shortbread," said Lady Farrington. "And some tea. It's good for shock."

"Thank you," said Peggy, accepting a crumbly triangle. Jed took one, too. His ankle was wrapped in a neat white bandage. Her Ladyship, who volunteered at a military hospital, said it was sprained, not broken.

"Thank you for explaining everything," went on Lady Farrington. "I can only deeply apologise for the appalling behaviour of my nephew."

"Aunty, I was never going to actually *hurt* them," protested her nephew, sitting in the far corner of the drawing room. It turned out the gas mask belonged to the boy they'd first seen in the back of the red Roadster. He was soggier now, and a lot less self-important.

"I told *you* to hush, Edmund," snapped Her Ladyship. "I am very close to calling the constable. You have terrorised two children from my village and that is unforgivable."

"We didn't actually *steal* the money," Peggy insisted.

"It was finders, keepers," said Jed.

"Quite right!" said Lady Farrington. "Anyone stupid enough to bury money in a bog should expect to lose it. Have you been taking money from my safe again, Edmund?"

"I was only *borrowing* it," whined Edmund, with no trace of American accent now. "I owe some money to another chap at school and – "

"Enough," said Lady Farrington. "I'm going to telephone your father and ask him to drive back and get you. I don't think I want you staying here for a week, after all. Who knows what else you might decide to pilfer?"

Edmund went pale. "Please … please don't call Father."

"It's your father or the constable," said his aunt. "Take your pick."

He sagged. "Father, then, I suppose."

"Fine. Off you go and pack."

Edmund stood up.

"Wait," said Lady Farrington. "Don't you have something to say to Peggy and Jed?"

Edmund's face creased. "Look here – I'm sorry, you two. I really never meant to scare you quite so badly. I was just … desperate. A chap has to pay his debts. Please forgive me."

Peggy and Jed looked at each other, shrugged and nodded.

"Thank you, Edmund," said Lady Farrington. "Off you go."

Her Ladyship walked them back to the gates. Properly bandaged, Jed could hobble quite well. As they passed the Austin, still skewed across the driveway, Lady Farrington said: "Taking *my car* for his dirty dealings, too! I'm very much regretting allowing Edmund's father to teach him to drive on the estate.

She took a breath. "Of course, if you want to go to the constable, you absolutely should," she said. "It will be a ghastly embarrassment for the family, but that's too bad."

Peggy and Jed glanced at each other.

"It seems like he's sorry – " said Peggy.

"Hmmm," said Her Ladyship. "He certainly will be when his father gets here."

"What about your money?" asked Jed.

"As you said – finders, keepers," said Lady Farrington with a firm nod. "No doubt your families can use it."

"Jed's father got injured in an air raid," said Peggy. "He can't get enough work now, so I want Jed to have it all."

"No," said Jed, flushing pink. "Half and half!"

"I wonder ... is your father good with horses?" asked Her Ladyship.

"He used to drive the horse and cart for the dairy," said Jed. "He loves horses."

"One of my grooms has been called up to join the Navy. So, I might have a job for him, if he can get about."

"Dad *can* get about!" said Jed. "He just can't sit up on the cart all day, like he used to."

"Then do ask him to come and see me tomorrow," said Lady Farrington. "Now – hurry home before your families start to worry. I hope I will see you both at the Metal Weigh-In on Saturday."

Peggy shrugged. "We've got hardly any. My brothers will get heaps, though. They'll just laugh at us when we turn up with what we've got."

Lady Farrington suddenly stopped. She looked left and right and then turned a full circle, a thoughtful frown on her fine features. "I have an idea," she said.

That Saturday, Arthur and Bill stood outside Tedbury Parish Hall with a colossal pile of old oil cans, two garden gates, a bike frame, drainpipes, a camping stove, corrugated iron and – right on top – the stolen pram.

Gary Smedley and Richie Carter had a pile almost as high. The local Scouts had worked in twos, threes and fours, depositing mound after mound of scrap metal in the town square.

Peggy and Jed's wheelbarrow contained the corrugated iron panel, the two metal brackets, the bent bicycle wheel and a dozen or so bottle-tops.

"Nice try," chortled Arthur, while Bill just laughed and shook his head at their pathetic haul.

A local grain merchant had set up a huge weighing platform on the council steps. An open-topped lorry was parked up against it. Each metal pile was weighed and registered by Lady Farrington and a parish councillor, before the platform tilted and the metal clattered into the lorry.

Jed and Peggy stepped up last with their offering. The dial on the scales barely moved. There was laughter in the crowd. Some of it kindly.

Peggy nodded to Jed and they both faced the square.

"We couldn't bring all of it," Jed said. "But the rest will be coming in the week."

"Awww ... are you going to collect some more bottle-tops?" chortled Arthur.

"No," said Jed.

"But we *have* collected – " said Peggy, "two 16-foot wrought-iron gates and half a mile of wrought-iron fencing."

There was a moment of hush followed by disbelieving laughter.

Then Lady Farrington stepped forward. "I can confirm Peggy and Jed's contribution," she declared. "They both persuaded me to donate the decorative iron fencing along the driveway to Farrington House *and* the wrought-iron gates of the main entrance. Until their visit this week, such a thought had never occurred to me."

The audience gaped and then applause broke out. Peggy watched her brothers' jaws drop. Then Bill started clapping, too. He elbowed Arthur until Arthur joined in.

There was no doubt who had won. Who would get a ride in a tank. Who would get a medal and a ten-shilling note. But watching her brothers realise what their little sister and her friend had achieved was the BEST reward ever.

Peggy might even let them ride in the tank, too, if Jed agreed.

Then Lady Farrington walked up to the large poster which read: ALL BOYS CAN HELP. She pulled a strip of paper from her handbag and pinned it over those four words:

ALL BOYS ***AND GIRLS*** CAN HELP.

BONUS
Wartime women

Although women had been brought up to stay at home and do housework or look after children, with so many men away fighting in the war, there were jobs that had to be done.

From 1941, women took on important war work, quickly learning to be mechanics, engineers, munitions workers, air raid wardens, bus and ambulance drivers and fire fighters.

Around 80,000 women joined the Land Army, working hard on farms to keep the country fed.

More than 640,000 women joined the armed forces, too.

Some women learned to fly warplanes. Although they did not fly in battle, it was their job to fly planes to airfields where they were needed.

And around 60 women were spies, sent behind enemy lines to bring back crucial information to help win the war.

It's not surprising that when the war was over, women were no longer content to stay at home. The big push for equal rights for women and girls really began after the Second World War.

About the author

Did you always want to be an author?

No! I wanted to be a singer and actor and be in big shows. But I always loved writing, just for fun, and eventually I ended up writing for my job, as a newspaper reporter. Then as a broadcast journalist for the BBC. Then I got into writing children's books and it's the BEST job.

Ali Sparkes

What's your favourite thing about being an author?

I love coming up with ideas and then getting to write them and share them with readers all over the world.

How did you come up with the idea for this book?

Where I live, in Southampton, England, we have a civic centre building with low walls all around it. The walls are only about 20 centimetres high and all the kids like to run along them – including me, when I was a kid … and today! The reason the walls are so low is that there used to be iron railings set into them, but during the Second World War, these were removed and melted down to make tanks and warships. I was wondering about this and different aspects of the war effort. I was also interested (and a bit annoyed) about how Boy Scouts were always getting involved, but no posters called for help from girls! I wanted to write about a girl who felt like I did and proved herself to be as good as the boys.

Are any of the characters based on people you know?
Not anyone in particular, but I meet brave, bold children in schools quite a lot. I know loads of them would want to step up and help!

Does anything relate to your own experiences?
Playing in the woods with a friend is what I did when I was the same age as Peggy and Jed. I knew all the paths around the woods and how to make bridges over the streams and build dens in the bushes. It was lovely to write about that.

What do you know about wartime Britain?
I wasn't alive during wartime but my parents remember growing up after the war, when there wasn't much food and people still had to use ration books. I asked my mum about eating things like sheep's hearts and she told me they tasted all right but were really rubbery to chew.

What do you hope readers will get from the book?
I think it's important to help out. If your community needs everyone (boys and girls) to pull together for a good reason, you should get involved. When we do things together, we can really make a difference. Recycling metal in the war is a lot like our recycling today. Both are really important for our future.

Is there anything else you want readers to do?
Have you tried bread pudding? It's soooo nice. See if you can get some at a bakery. Or make some at home!

About the illustrator

Did you always want to be an illustrator?

Yes! Well, I wanted to be a comic artist when I was 10 years old. I made my own comic books and my friends would read them.

Chita Erayanie

How did you get into illustrating?

Although I studied art at university, I didn't know much about illustrating a story. So I took a short course where I learned about creating characters and environments. We created a dummy book, and my character was an activist during the Civil Rights Movement in America called Jo Ann Robinson. The whole process was really exciting and that was when I knew I wanted to do more of this.

Do you use pens and paints or do you work digitally?

I work with both! I start with sketches using pencils, then decide if I want to colour them digitally or manually. If I choose manual work, I usually work with watercolour, gouache, and pastels. I think both skills are nice to have.

What was your favourite scene to illustrate?

The kitchen where Peggy, her mother and brother are having a conversation. I enjoyed drawing the vintage kitchen and the old-style cookware.

Do you do lots of research for historical scenes?
Definitely! Research is actually one of my favourite parts when illustrating historical fiction books. I have a folder full of images of gas masks, vintage cars, women's fashion in the 1940s, and Anderson shelters. I had never heard of an Anderson shelter before but now I know how people back then built them! I always learn something new from my research.

Which character in the book did you identify with the most?
Maybe Peggy's brothers because me and my sister used to pick on our youngest sister (we fought all the time but now we're best friends!). Also, because I used to be in the Scouts like Peggy's brothers. We didn't help any war effort, but we often helped clean our neighbourhood streets.

Which character was the most fun to draw?
I loved drawing the boy in the gas mask. Instead of a face, I drew big goggles and a snout. It was supposed to be scary but when he fell in the stream and got soaked he looked so pitiful and funny.

Were you surprised by any of the facts about wartime Britain?
Yes! I'm not British and I just moved to the UK a few years ago so I'm still learning a lot about the country's history. From this book I found out that people collected metal from fences, pots, pans, and prams to be melted down and reused for military purposes. I even found a photo online of men standing on a huge pile of pots and pans!

Book chat

When you saw the book title, what did you think the book might be about? Were you right?

Do you have a favourite part of the story?

What do you think about girls not being allowed to help initially?

What do you know about this time in history?

Do any of the characters change from the start of the story to the end?

If you could speak to the author, what would you ask?

How would you sum up this book in just three words?

Who would you recommend this book to and why?

Book challenge:

Design your own poster inviting people to help with a cause of your choice.

Published by Collins
An imprint of HarperCollins*Publishers*

The News Building
1 London Bridge Street
London
SE1 9GF
UK

Macken House
39/40 Mayor Street Upper
Dublin 1
D01 C9W8
Ireland

Text © Ali Sparkes 2025
Design and illustrations © HarperCollins*Publishers* Limited 2025

10 9 8 7 6 5 4 3 2 1

ISBN 978-0-00-876786-0

All rights reserved. No part of this publication may be reproduced, stored in a retrieval system, or transmitted in any form by any means, electronic, mechanical, photocopying, recording or otherwise, without the prior written permission of the Publisher or a licence permitting restricted copying in the United Kingdom issued by the Copyright Licensing Agency Ltd, 5th Floor, Shackleton House, 4 Battle Bridge Lane, London SE1 2HX.

Without limiting the exclusive rights of any author, contributor or the publisher of this publication, any unauthorised use of this publication to train generative artificial intelligence (AI) technologies is expressly prohibited. HarperCollins also exercise their rights under Article 4(3) of the Digital Single Market Directive 2019/790 and expressly reserve this publication from the text and data mining exception.

British Library Cataloguing-in-Publication Data
A catalogue record for this publication is available from the British Library.

Download the teaching notes and word cards to accompany this book at:
http://littlewandle.org.uk/signupfluency/

Get the latest Collins Big Cat news at
collins.co.uk/collinsbigcat

Author: Ali Sparkes
Illustrator: Chita Erayanie (Illo Agency)
Publisher: Laura White
Product manager and
 commissioning editor: Caroline Green
Series editor: Charlotte Raby
Development editor: Catherine Baker
Project manager: Emily Hooton
Copyeditor: Sally Byford
Proofreader: Catherine Dakin
Cover designer: Sarah Finan
Typesetter: 2Hoots Publishing Services Ltd
Production controller: Katharine Willard

Printed in the UK.

 **MIX**
Paper | Supporting responsible forestry
FSC™ C007454

This book contains FSC™ certified paper and other controlled sources to ensure responsible forest management.

For more information visit: www.harpercollins.co.uk/green

Made with responsibly sourced paper and vegetable ink

Scan to see how we are reducing our environmental impact.

Acknowledgements
The publishers gratefully acknowledge the permission granted to reproduce the copyright material in this book. Every effort has been made to trace copyright holders and to obtain their permission for the use of copyright material. The publishers will gladly receive any information enabling them to rectify any error or omission at the first opportunity.

p20 The National Archives/Getty Images, p21 The National Archives/Getty Images, p37c Tang Yan Song/Shutterstock, p37b Chronicle/Alamy, p37t Everett Collection Inc/Alamy, p54 Kevin Wheal/Alamy, p55t Axel Bueckert/Alamy, p55b Photo 12/Getty Images, p70 Neil McAllister/Alamy, p71 Harry Todd/Getty Images, p104bl Pictorial Press Ltd/Alamy, p104br Smith Archive/Alamy, p105 Shawshots/Alamy.